BUFFY
THE BUTTERFLY

TED LANDKAMMER

Copyright © 2022 **Ted Landkammer**

All rights reserved. No part of this publication may be reproduced, distributed, or transmitted in any form or by any means, including photocopying, recording, or other electronic or mechanical methods, without the prior written permission of the publisher, except in the case of brief quotations embodied in critical reviews and certain other noncommercial uses permitted by copyright law. For permission requests, write to the publisher, addressed "Attention: Book Rights and Permission," at the address below.

Published in the United States of America

ISBN 978-1-958518-18-2 (HC)

Ted Landkammer
222 West 6th Street
Suite 400, San Pedro, CA, 90731
www.stellarliterary.com

Order Information and Rights Permission:

Quantity sales. Special discounts might be available on quantity purchases by corporations, associations, and others. For details, contact the publisher at the address above.

For Book Rights Adaptation and other Rights Permission. Call us at toll-free 1-888-945-8513 or send us an email at admin@stellarliterary.com.

Table Of Contents

Title

Copyright

Dedication

Story Start

About the Author

To my three children: Elizabeth, Mark, and Melissa.

From Dad.

And from Grandpa to Emily, Blake, Noel, Ben, Isabella, and Sophia.

Many, many stories were told to all of you.

This one was especially liked by my granddaughters Emily Weber and Noel Landkammer.

Thanks to the illustrators for their wonderful creations and inspirations which were used in the original first draft as follows:

Melissa Solito for the butterfly and rose on the drafts of the front and back covers.

Helen Hanson for the drafts of the pink hotel (Royal Hawaiian) and for "fat" Buffy.

Steve Hanson for the Buffy cocoons and Jake the Giraffe drafts.

Emily Weber for drafts of Buffy in his rocking chair and Buffy in the jungle.

Buffy was in his cocoon, hanging upside down on a chickaree tree. These trees grow in Africa, and Buffy would start his life there. Buffy started to wriggle his way out of the cocoon, and he said, "I wonder what the world is like?"

Then out came his head and then a wing and then another, and he found himself sitting on a branch. All Buffy could see was green leaves and the trunks of trees.

"So this is the world," said Buffy. "All green, green, and brown." But then he looked up, and there was a big patch of blue. "Oh, what is that?" said Buffy. "That must be the sky. I heard about that once in a lullaby."

Buffy flew up to the top branch and perched there, looking up at all the blue. "It's so big," said Buffy.

"No." Laughed Jake. "I only eat leaves and grass." But, just then, Jake took a big bite of leaves and shook the branch Buffy was on so hard that he fell to the ground.

"Sorry, little fellow," Jake said. And he bent down to the ground, saying, "Climb up on one of my horns, and I'll take you to visit my friend."

Jake took off running, his long legs covering so much ground and new sights flashing by that Buffy clung to Jake's horn with all his might. In fact, Buffy was shouting, "Please, slow down." But Jake's hooves were making so much noise when hitting the ground that he couldn't hear Buffy.

"What a world this is and what new things to see!"

Just then, Jake galloped over a small hill, and then Buffy saw a strange sight. Some great big animals were standing in a pond and spraying one another with something that Buffy had never seen before.

"Who, who are they?" stammered Buffy, kind of frightened. "And what is that they are in?"

"Well," Jake said, "that is water, and these are my friends, the elephants."

"My very special friend is Effie." And Jake introduced Effie to Buffy, saying, "This is my friend, Buffy the butterfly."

"Gee willikers," said Buffy to Effie. "You are big!"

"Yes," Effie said, "we are the largest animals in the jungle." Buffy flew up on Effie the elephant's back, and Effie took him for a ride. "Was that a good ride?" asked Effie.

"Yes," said Buffy, "but what do you guys do for fun?"

"Oh," said Jake, "we have our own band, and we play for the other animals, and sometimes they all gather in a circle and dance and sing. You see, I play cymbals, and Molee the monkey plays drums, and Effie the elephant plays piano, and Lennie the lion plays the trumpet."

"Oh," said Buffy. "I'd like to play. What could I play?" asked Buffy. Effie said, "We need someone to play the reed horn."

"Reed horn," said Buffy. "What is that?"

"Well, it's two sawgrass reeds tied to a stick, and by blowing on it, you get a singing sound," Jake said. "Yes, you could fan your wings against the reed horn."

"Great," said Buffy. "When can we play?"

Effie answered, "We will play tonight after our naps and when the moon comes out."

Buffy and all of the animals gathered in the elephant's campground at dark. Effie said, "Here, Buffy, I made you a reed horn from the sawgrass." Buffy blew on it, and out came a sound that scared Buffy at first. Then he got used to it and started making all kinds of music on the reeds. It was great! They all played until midnight and danced and had a grand time.

Buffy went to sleep high in an African willow tree until he heard the elephants spraying water on their backs in the watering hole. "What a sight and what a world," said Buffy. "I would like to see more of it."

That morning Buffy asked Jake and Effie what else there was to see in the world. Effie said her cousin Bubbaroo was in a circus in Hawaii, and they heard that Hawaii was lots of fun to see.

"But how would I get there?" asked Buffy.

Jake the giraffe said, "I know how. Just over chat mountain is the boat harbor of Moronga. You could fly onboard and hide in one of the lifeboats. But first, you must make sure the boat is going to Hawaii."

At that and wanting very much to see more of the world, Buffy said thanks to all his friends and told them he hoped to see them again. "Bye," said Buffy, and off he flew over the mountain to the port of Moronga. Buffy soon saw a big boat in the harbor which had a sign on it saying Loading for Hawaii. "Great," said Buffy, and he flew high above the boat's smokestacks and settled on a lifeboat near the front of the ship. He crawled down through a small hole in the boat's tarp and hid there. Soon, Buffy heard the sound of the boat's horn and heard the captain shout, "All aboard!"

"What a great feeling," said Buffy. 'I'm off to see more of the world."

All the passengers rushed for the gangway and settled aboard. Buffy saw many of them waving to people on shore. Then he felt the big ship move, and before long, the port of Moronga was just a speck in the distance.

"This is exciting," said Buffy. "Lots of people to watch from my perch on the lifeboat and plenty of things to eat." You see, at night when it was dark, Buffy would fly into the cook's kitchen and munch on crumbs and things left behind. In fact, Buffy ate so much that his tummy got real big by the time they reached Hawaii! He was so big, he could barely fly.

After eight days sailing, Buffy was getting anxious to get back on solid ground. He was getting his sea legs all right, but Buffy was ready to lie on the sandy beaches he had heard about. And he wanted to see a hula dance.

Buffy went to sleep under the lifeboat canvas, and then something jolted him awake. Then he heard the captain shouting, "All ashore, what's going ashore." Buffy saw the people and the little children going down the gangplank. And Buffy joined them by flying out and landing on a man's big cop hat.

After riding atop the man's big hat on down the gangplank, Buffy took off flying and flew to a grove of trees standing next to a big pink hotel. "Gee willikers," said Buffy. "I can't believe the size of that building!" Buffy strained his neck but couldn't even see to the top of the big pink building.

While looking upward, Buffy heard a squeak. Buffy jumped. "Who are you?" asked Buffy.

"I am Missy the Mouse, and my house is in this tree."

"Oh, I would like to see your house," said Buffy.

"Well, come along," said Missy the Mouse." "I have a lovely Hawaiian house."

Sure enough, just inside a big hole in the tree was the mouse's house. "Very comfortable," said Buffy. There was a chair and table, a big pile of nuts the mouse chewed on, and a very soft bed of dried grass. The bed was curved like a cradle and was part of a palm tree. "I would love to have a soft bed made out of a palm tree," said Buffy.

Missy the Mouse asked Buffy what he was doing in Hawaii, and Buffy said he wanted to see everything he could in Hawaii, including the Hula girls. "Well," said the mouse, "you are in luck. They do the hula every evening on the stage at the big pink hotel. You can come with me tonight." Missy the Mouse said, "And maybe you can even do the hula."

"How could I do that?" asked Buffy. "I have nothing to wear."

"No problem," said the mouse. "I have a small hula outfit I made that you can wear!" And the mouse dug into a strange box and pulled out a bright red grass hula skirt.

That night, they went over to the stage, and big lights came on, and the music started. The hula dancers were beautiful, and after a while, they encouraged others to come up on the stage. "This is your chance," said the mouse. "Quick, put on your hula outfit and get on the stage."

Buffy was a bit frightened, but he flew up on the stage and started to hula. "Hooray," said the mouse. "You look great!"

Buffy did the hula for quite a while until one little girl tried to grab him, and then he flew up into a tree. The mouse scrambled up to join him, and the mouse was still laughing.

And then Buffy started laughing, saying, "Wasn't it grand? Wasn't it a lot of fun?"

"You were the hit of the night," said the mouse.

They went back to mouse's house, and being tired, they soon went to sleep.

In the morning, Buffy bid farewell to Missy the Mouse, thanking her for the use of her home and for the hula skirt and the dancing. The mouse asked Buffy, "Where are you going now?"

"I am going to fly around the island and see the sights, and then I would like to visit another country. You see, I am a world traveler!"

When Buffy had finished all his world travels, he settled back down in Africa with all his friends. He had grown a long gray beard, and he liked to sit in his rocking chair and tell his grandchildren the stories of his world travels. His stories were fun. And not only did all of his grandchildren sit quietly and listen, but his friend the blue bird, which everyone called Mark the Lark, would listen. And his friend, the golden tailed squirrel called Lib-Rib, would join for the story.

Then after the stories, they would all join hands and do a dance to the music of Jake the Giraffe, Effie the Elephant, Lennie the Lion, and Molee the Monkey.